Marianna Burgess Embe

Stiya

A Carlisle Indian Girl at Home

Marianna Burgess Embe

Stiya
A Carlisle Indian Girl at Home

ISBN/EAN: 9783337413842

Printed in Europe, USA, Canada, Australia, Japan

Cover: Foto ©Raphael Reischuk / pixelio.de

More available books at **www.hansebooks.com**

STIYA

A CARLISLE INDIAN GIRL AT HOME

*FOUNDED ON THE AUTHOR'S ACTUAL
OBSERVATIONS*

By EMBE

CAMBRIDGE
Printed at the Riverside Press
1891

To

TONKÈ,

WHO SHARED THE PLEASURES AND SORROWS OF A TRIP
AMONG THE PUEBLOS, THIS LITTLE BOOK IS
LOVINGLY DEDICATED BY

THE AUTHOR.

THE story of Stiya and her trials is woven out of the experiences of girls at various times members of the Indian Industrial School at Carlisle, Pa. The fundamental facts, therefore, are true. Different Indian villages have contributed incidents and served for the pueblo of the story. Through persons connected with the school the brutal governor who figures in the story was reported to the Government at Washington. The Indian Department sent out a special agent to investigate the matter, and finding the facts of the public indignity substantially as related, the governor was arrested and lodged in jail. This circumstance gives those interested in Indian education the hope that a brighter day may now be dawning, when the home conditions will be so changed that there will be no more tribal tyranny, but all will be under the protection and enjoy the privileges of our good Government.

CONTENTS AND LIST OF ILLUSTRATIONS.

STIYA:

OR, A CARLISLE INDIAN GIRL AT HOME.

CHAPTER I.

DISAPPOINTMENT.

WHEN I was told at Carlisle that I could go to
my home in the West — a place I had not seen for
five years — I was truly delighted ; and all the time
I was packing my trunk, and all the way while we,
a merry party of forty Indian girls and boys, all
going home, were laughing and having a good time,
at every thought of home and mother and father
and the friends I should find on my arrival, my
heart gave a great thump of joy.

After five days and nights of travel, every mile of which I enjoyed, for we were so very comfortable in the cars, and we saw so many interesting things which then I could understand about, in the middle of one hot afternoon the train stopped at the station at which I was to get off, and I realized that I was at the end of my railroad journey.

My father and mother, who were at the station waiting for their daughter, rushed in my direction as soon as they saw me, and talking Indian as fast as they could tried to help me from the train.

My father took my valise, and my mother, seizing me by the arm, threw her head upon my shoulder and cried for joy.

Was I as glad to see them as I thought I would be?

I must confess that instead I was shocked and surprised at the sight that met my eyes.

" *My* father ? *My* mother ? " cried I desperately within. " No, never ! " I thought, and I actually turned my back upon them.

I had forgotten that home Indians had such grimy faces.

I had forgotten that my mother's hair always looked as though it had never seen a comb.

I had forgotten that she wore such a short, queer-looking black bag for a dress, fastened over one shoulder only, and such buckskin wrappings for shoes and leggings.

" My mother ? " I cried, this time aloud.

I could not help it, and at the same time I rushed frantically into the arms of my *school*-mother, who had taken me home, and I remembered then as I never did before how kind she had always been to us. I threw my arms around her neck and cried bitterly, and begged of her to let me get on the train again.

"I cannot go with that woman," I pleaded.

My school-mother, in a voice so tender I shall never forget, said, "My dear girl, you must stop crying. You must not feel in this way towards your own parents. This is your mother. She loves you. You will get used to her ways by and by. Come, now," she continued, trying to withdraw from my embrace, "be a woman! Make the best of these people, and go to your mother. Go, *now*, to your mother. Shake hands with her as a dutiful daughter should."

Almost broken hearted, I did as I was bid, for I knew nothing else than to obey my school-mother.

I also took my father's hand, and through my tears smiled as best I could; but he never shall know how I suffered with mortification and regret that he was such an Indian.

Somehow, I had my mind made up that my par-

ents would be different, and it was hard for me to
realize that they had been going backward while I
had been going forward for five years.

By this time the locomotive bell began to ring,
and my school-mother stepped aboard the train.

Soon she and the coach full of school companions
I had left passed out of sight, and as I gazed after
them, my eyes thoroughly blinded with tears, my
heart felt heavy with sadness.

"Oh, my! Oh, my!" I sighed; "what have I
come to?"

My home being ten miles from the station, a
burro, which seemed to me then hardly larger than
a rat, indeed so small that I was afraid I should
crush him if I got on his back, was brought to take
me home. I had forgotten about these useful hard-
workers, but badly treated creatures.

Climbing on his back in a way that I felt to be

very awkward, I could not help laughing, in which my mother and others standing near joined, but when they began to pile my trunk on behind me, and my mother mounted in front of me, I laughed more.

"Can such a little creature carry all this load?" I asked.

No answer. I had unconsciously spoken in English. Indeed, I could not speak much Indian, and as my father and mother knew no English, my ride home was almost a silent one as far as I was concerned, but my father and mother talked as they rode along, my father on another burro at our side.

I listened carefully to see if the Indian words would not come back to me, and some of them did.

I understood enough to know that they were talking about my money, and white lady, and my dress, and how big I had grown.

My father looked a great deal at me, and once he reached across and stroked my arm and said, " My daughter."

This made me want to cry again. But I did not. The words of my school-mother, " Be a woman," rang in my ears, and I tried to tell father in part Indian and part English that I was glad to get back.

Before we reached home I grew very tired.

When I saw the village in the distance, I was glad; and as we rode to what I knew must be our house, I was more than ready to get off the donkey's back.

Our house was made of sand and mud-brick, called adobe, and was built on the top of another house.

I thought that may be my father would have a new house built, with a door on the ground floor;

but no, we had to climb a ladder to get into our
house, the same as we did before I went to school.

The ladder was high and the rounds far apart
and loose, so I was almost afraid to get on them, but
there was no other way.

My mother went first.

I ascended the ladder behind my mother, but I
assure you not with the same grace.

I succeeded in gaining the top, however, with
much less trouble than I had anticipated.

CHAPTER II.

MY HOME.

THE landing at the top of the ladder was the flat roof of the house underneath ours.

This roof had been covered with dirt, which had in time become thoroughly packed and almost as hard as flagging, so it really formed a stone-like balcony to our house.

There was no railing around it, and I don't see how the Indians manage to keep their babies from falling from the tops of these houses. There are many in the village just like ours, and in many there are more children than at our house.

There were only six of us children, every one of

whom, except myself, died when quite small of the small-pox and diphtheria, and at the time of which I am writing I wished that I had gone with the rest.

On reaching the top of the ladder and looking backward, I saw my father with another Indian, whom he had called to help carry my trunk up the ladder, tugging with all their might.

As I stood watching them I could not help thinking of the time I went to Carlisle. It did not then require two men to carry my things, for everything I owned in the way of wearing apparel was on my back, and it was very scant at that.

" Why, father, you cannot get the trunk through that small door," said I in despair, as they approached the entrance to the house.

He understood what I said, and smiling seemed to think it was doubtful, but by hard pushing and considerable scratching they managed to get it inside.

By the time the trunk, the man who helped my
father carry the trunk, my father, my mother, and
myself got well into the little twelve by fourteen
room, which was the only room our house could
boast of, you can imagine it was exceedingly full.

My father seated himself upon the trunk, the Indian upon a block of wood, while my mother busied
herself about the fire, and I looked around to see
where my hat and coat could be hung, and in which
corner to put my hand valise.

The ceiling of the room was so low that by standing on tip-toe I could reach it. It was very black
with age and smoke as well as very dirty, being the
under part of the flat roof, which was made of grass
and mud thrown over poles a foot apart laid cross-
wise, leaving apertures a foot square through which
the dry chips and dirt were continually dropping.

The ceiling was a splendid place, too, for wasps

and spiders to build nests, and they had done good work during my absence.

Besides that, I well remembered when a child seeing an occasional scorpion, centipede, or tarantula drop to the floor from that very same roof, and how we used to jump about to find something to kill it with. Once a snake was seen crawling along one of the poles and was killed, making fine fun for us children.

"Well," sighed I, "this is still my home, is it? No improvement upon what it was when I went away? Then I was a child, now I am a young woman. Here is where I am to stay, is it? Will it ever be different? Can I stand it? Shall I try to?"

All these and a hundred other questions crowded upon my mind in the few minutes spent in looking around.

PUEBLO CHILDREN

I found another block of wood and sat down, not offering to help my mother get supper, for I was dreadfully tired, and I knew she would rather do the work herself that first night.

The fire-place was built in the corner of the room, and looked very much like the fire-place in any house.

A chimney made of stone and adobe brick carried off most of the smoke.

My mother, after making the fire, took down a piece of meat from a line.

It was mutton, and had been cut very thin and hung up on the line to dry, as people in civilized countries hang their clothes on lines to dry.

The line was stretched across the room from side to side, and was full of meat.

Flies?

If I should say that a million flies flew from the

meat when my mother shook the line you would think that I was not telling the truth, but there were certainly thousands upon thousands of them.

But, then, *that* was nothing.

My father and mother and the visiting Indian did n't care how many flies roosted upon the meat, so that they did not eat it up, and they did n't.

The piece that my mother tore off was about as large as two dinner plates and as thin.

This she broke up into smaller pieces and pounded with a stone into quite fine threads, and then she put it into a stew pan and stewed it.

The stew, with tea and some Indian bread baked the day before, made up our supper.

Had I not watched the supper being prepared, had it been placed on a table instead of on the floor at our feet, I might have felt like eating.

I was hungry, but could not eat; and excusing

myself with a headache went outside and stood on
the balcony (?), stood there in the bright moonlight
and pure clear air, and thought.

All was still as death.

There were no lights in any of the houses.

In the moonlight I could see human beings
stretched on blankets on the tops of adjoining
houses.

They thus come out in the cool air to sleep and
escape the vermin inside of their filthy abodes.

I know not how long I stood there, thinking,
thinking, oh, I cannot tell what, so much passed
through my mind, and I was so desperately homesick for Carlisle; but I was awakened finally from
my reverie by my father and the man with him coming from the room.

They did not seem to notice me, for which I was
thankful, but descended the ladder and passed out
of sight.

Then I went into the house, found my mother had pushed the dishes back in the corner with the general heap by the fire-place, and was placing blankets on the floor ready for the night.

The light in the room was poor, only that which the few burning sticks on the fire-place gave out.

The room was full of tobacco smoke, my father and the Indian with him having smoked several cigarettes after supper, and there were odors of meat and supper enough to stifle one, but there was only one window, which was rarely ever opened, and the door and the fire-place for ventilation.

My mother was a small woman and very quick in her movements, so she soon had the beds ready.

Mine, I could see, was given an extra blanket or two and a soft sheepskin.

It was made in the corner of the room farthest from my father's and mother's bed.

CHAPTER III.

UNSETTLED.

My father soon returned. After smoking another cigarette, and talking a few minutes, he curled down in his nest for the night.

Neither my father nor mother minded the thick air, and were soon sound asleep.

How I did want a bath before going to bed, and as I wished, again the memory of the first night at Carlisle came to me. How they put me into a large bath-tub, combed my hair, and put me to bed between two clean white sheets. I did not appreciate the kind treatment then.

Then I was lonesome for this very place that now I was loathing with all my heart.

As I lay on the hard floor, for all the blankets they gave me and the sheepskin did not seem to make it soft, — as I lay there, not a wink of sleep coming to my tired eyes, I thought and discussed and planned thus : —

"Would that I had never been at school !

"Would I had never learned better ways. It makes it harder for me to endure this life now."

A moment after I heard myself saying, "I do not wish anything of the kind. I am glad I went away to school. I would not take the world for what I learned at dear old Carlisle.

"No, indeed! I have so much at least, and no one can ever take away from me what I have learned.

"But, oh ! oh ! this horrid smoke !

"This dreadful air. My head ! my head ! It will surely burst."

I tossed and turned from one side of my hard

bed to the other, thinking one minute that schools were a good thing for the Indians, and the next moment thinking they were not.

"Yes, they are of use, especially those far away from our homes," I concluded.

"I never in the world would have learned to be disgusted at this way of living, had I not been taken clear away from it, where I could not see it, nor hear anything about it for years.

"Some people think for that very reason schools away from home are not so good as schools at home.

"They think we ought to stay near to this filth, this dirt. I suppose they think it is good enough for us. Thank God, however, there are some people who think we should have as good a chance as children of other races.

"I am thankful I had a chance to get away from this, if only for a little while.

" We *must* learn to feel disgust for these things. If we have no disgust for them we will never try to make them better.

" We MUST be disgusted, I say, and I *am* thoroughly disgusted this moment at the way the Indians live, if *this* is the way they live. I know, however, that some live in great deal worse houses than this.

" I can make this place better.

" I must make home more pleasant.

" But, pshaw! What is the use?

" My mother don't care. My father is satisfied with things as they are.

" I don't care if he is satisfied, *I* am not, and there MUST be a change. I will show them a better way of living than this.

" But they will not listen. They will make fun of me, I know."

And thus I plunged and struggled, asserting and contradicting myself, until, worn out and nervous, I sat up in bed, and bringing my fist down upon my knee, said almost in despair : —

" I cannot stay, that is all there is about it. I simply cannot stay here."

Then the next moment I found myself saying, " I MUST stay." Then again, " I MUST go back. I am not through with my studies. I want to graduate. I MUST graduate," and the thought of last Commencement day at Carlisle, the class of boys and girls who received their diplomas from the hands of the Secretary of the Interior himself — how manly the boys looked! how sweet and pretty and womanly the girls! All this flashed through my mind.

I said unconsciously, " I want to be in such a class some day. I *will* belong to a Carlisle gradu-

ating class some day." And then I saw the crowds
of visitors and experienced again the joyousness of
the whole day.

I forgot for the moment that I was at home, in
a corner of a filthy little room, lying on the floor,
but another throb of the head and my father's snor-
ing brought me back to the meat odors, the smoke,
the stifling air.

"I am not at Carlisle. I am here. I am at
home."

The words of my school-mother again said to me,
"Be a woman!"

I straightened myself down on my back, and
with hands lifted in air and clasped tightly, resolved
to try.

"Let me see! I have some money; how much?
Five — ten — fifteen, yes, when I counted it before
I left the cars I had forty-seven dollars.

"No, I cannot give them all that. I want to keep it.

"I will keep my money and say nothing about it," thought I.

CHAPTER IV.

THE first thing my father said the next morning was, " Have you any money ? "

" Yes, a little," I replied.

" How much ? " asked he eagerly, and my mother, who was folding up the bed-clothes, straightened up, and with arms akimbo stood looking intently at me to hear the amount.

" Forty-seven dollars," I replied, not daring to tell a lie.

They were both amazed at the amount. It seemed so much money for a girl to have all by herself.

"Where did you get it?" asked my mother, leaning toward me.

"I worked in a family for a while, and they paid me for my work."

"Did the man (meaning our superintendent) let you keep all that money yourself?"

"Of course he did. That is, he kept it in the bank for me, and gave it to me when I started home. Do you think he would keep my money for himself?"

My father and mother looked at each other in astonishment, as if a new truth had just dawned upon them.

"Why, what is the matter?" I asked.

"Well," said my father, affecting an air of indifference now, "the priest says that the man who has charge of the Carlisle school puts the children out on farms and then pockets the money they earn."

This aroused me.

"Nonsense," I exclaimed; "every boy and girl has his or her own money. Some of the boys have earned and put in bank as high as $200.

"We go to school, too, with white children when we are out in the country, and that is better than going to the Carlisle school, even if Carlisle is the very best Indian school in the world. Our superintendent always tells us it is better for us to get out away from Indians and among good people whose ways we want to try to learn."

I told them this, but they did not pay much attention. I am sure I did not speak very good Indian, but they seemed to understand what I said before.

My mother went on with her work of getting breakfast, and my father went out to attend to the burros.

After rolling up my bed as my mother did hers, I picked up the water-jar, went down the ladder and off to the spring for some fresh water.

This water-jar was an earthen vessel made by my mother's own hands.

She made it when I was a child. I remember going with her to get the clay.

We went nearly to the top of a high mesa to get it.

She mixed it with water and kneaded it like dough, and then she put in some crushed lava to make it stronger.

Then she shaped it with her hands into a big jar.

This one was large enough to hold two gallons of water.

When she had made it just the shape she wanted it, she set the jar out in the sun to dry. When it was dry she smeared it with white paint, and on the white she painted red and brown pictures of queer-looking animals with long legs and very big heads, and funny-looking birds and all sorts of mixed-up figures, and then she put it in a little oven to bake.

These vessels break very easily, but the Indian women and girls carry them full of water on their heads to and from the spring, and rarely ever break one.

I could run with mine on my head, and I never broke a water-jar in my life.

By the time I got back with the water, my father had returned and was eating his breakfast.

As the morning walk had given me an appetite, and not having seen the meal prepared, I ate a little, but when about half through, on turning around to get a drink of the water I had brought, I saw one of our lazy dogs that are always lying around the house lapping water from the jar.

PUEBLO WOMAN WITH WATER JAR

"Oh, dear! There it is again. Get out!" I cried, and my father drove the dog away, but not as I thought to do me a favor, but to get a drink himself. The dog is a part of the family, and my father considered him as clean as any member of the family, and no doubt he was.

But I could eat no more.

"Dogs up that ladder?" you say.

Yes, indeed. Some of the Pueblo dogs can climb ladders as well as people can. Our house was only on the top of ONE house, while some of them are piled up, one on top of the other, five or six houses high.

They don't look like the four and five story houses we see in large cities, because the roof of each house makes the balcony for the one above it; so, you see, they look like adobe terraces, and it is pretty hard to climb up to the fifth house over the

shaky ladders, with rounds so far apart that a child
can hardly reach from one to the other. But children and women and dogs and men go up and down
without the least trouble, and rarely ever fall.

I· do not believe that the Pueblo Indians have as
many dogs as some other tribes.

Why, I heard my Pawnee friend Minnie say one
day at school that their people have hundreds of
dogs.

" Where do they stay all the time, and what do
they eat ? " I asked.

" Oh," she said, " they stay in the tent with the
rest of us, and eat the same that we eat. Indeed,
many an old Indian woman has gone hungry that
the dogs might not starve. Don't your dogs stay in
the tent with you ? " she asked.

" We do not live in tents," I replied.

It seemed hard to make the girls understand

what kind of queer houses some of the Pueblos do live in.

"Our dogs come into the houses, though," I said, "but the place they like best to get into is the outside oven where we bake bread."

I did not see anything so very funny about that remark, but Minnie laughed heartily.

"The very idea," she said, "of dogs being in a bake oven!"

"Yes," I continued, "the ovens are like little houses with round roofs, and just the right size for five or six dogs.

"They look so comfortable in there, too, with their shaggy heads lying close to the little hole made to put the bread in. And they don't like to be disturbed either, when the bread has to be baked."

CHAPTER V.

THE WASHING.

A few days after I came home, I went with my mother down to the wash-hole, and this is the way she washed my father's trousers and shirt : —

There was a hollow place in the rock not far from our house.

There are many such places in the rock upon which our village was built, worn there by the action of the rains.

These holes and the footpaths to and from the spring and other places, worn in the solid stone, tell the story that our village must be hundreds of years old.

The water-holes during the season when it occa-
sionally rains are mostly full of water.

Sometimes the water in them gets stagnant and
foul and covered with a green scum, but it is never
considered too dirty to wash clothes in, and the Indians often drink from these slimy pools. Is it
much wonder that they get fevers and diphtheria
and other horrible diseases that visit unclean com-
munities of people ?

Is it any wonder that they die off by the hundred, as was the case this last year, in my own village ?

It was to one of these holes that I went with my
mother to help her wash.

I had some soiled garments of my own, and while
she washed my father's trousers and shirt, I washed
my own clothing.

We had no washboard, but were obliged to use

large stones, rubbing our clothes on them in the same way we do on washboards.

It is very hard work, though, to wash on one's knees, kneeling over with head nearly touching the water, and I found it very different from standing by the side of a washtub, where one has only to bend the back a little as one rubs.

But my mother did not seem to mind it.

I tried to do as she did, but got tired and impatient, and finally said, in not a very pleasant voice, —

"How can you stand this, mother? It makes me fairly dizzy, and nearly breaks my back."

My mother merely smiled.

"Do you know," I continued, "I can wash a whole half day, and do a big family wash, and not get half so tired as I feel this minute after only an hour's work."

PUEBLO WOMAN WASHING

Of course my mother did not know anything about "an hour." She measures time by the sun, but she looked at me sort of pitifully and said, " You will get used to it by and by."

" Get used to it ! " I exclaimed as I cast my eyes towards the clouds, " never ! I shall never wash this way again," and I never did.

My father wore white trousers, made of muslin.

They came only a very little below the knees, and, not being hemmed around the bottom, hung in natural fringe.

A man among civilized people would not be called dressed if he wore such trousers.

If he were walking in the streets of a city he would be arrested and put in jail.

Those men who can afford it wear buckskin leggings from the knee down, but many go bare-footed and bare-shinned.

The shirt is made of calico, and this with the trousers completes the costume of many.

Even the Governor of our village did not dress better.

He wore in addition, though, a lady's sundown, which must have seen much wet weather, and after every dampening received an extra poke in the top until it reached a peak, the height of an ordinary stove-pipe hat.

Imagine a peaked, straw stove-pipe with ragged rim and rusty, and you have the Governor's hat which he donned upon all occasions.

CHAPTER VI.

BROAD HINTS.

WHEN we went back to the house, my father, who was smoking his usual corn husk cigarette, said, "Let us go to the store this afternoon."

"How far is it?"

"About ten miles."

"Do you want to buy something?"

"Yes," he replied.

"All right," I answered, wondering at the same time if he really had any money.

"*You* want to buy something, too, don't you?" continued my father. "You see we are poor."

"Well," I replied. "My little money will not buy

much," thinking he meant me to buy something for the house.

"Let us go and see what they have at the store, anyway," he said.

"I will go, of course. I would *like* to go. Will you let me buy with my money what I want to?"

My mother said in reply, "They have nice shawls at the store."

"And lots of pretty coral beads and buckskin for moccasins and leggings," said my father.

"I saw some Moqui gowns there, too, like this," said my mother, looking down at her black robe. "You know a dress like this never wears out."

"Yes, I know, and I think it is wonderful how the Moqui Indians make such strong goods. They beat the white people. Some cloth made by white manufacturers is so tender it does not wear a year. But you have a Moqui dress. You don't want two, do you?"

"No, I do not need another," she replied while putting on her moccasins and leggings. "You know I gave your dress away when you went to school?"

I watched my mother put on her shoes, for I had almost forgotten how she did it; but when I saw her winding yards and yards of buckskin around her ankles and saw how very neatly she did it, not a wrinkle showing in all that great winding, I remembered well, but I thought she had the funniest, clumsiest looking ankles I ever saw.

Her ankles when wrapped were as thick and as straight as hitching posts.

I could not help wondering if I should ever wear such shoes again.

Then, all of a sudden, it dawned upon me what my father and mother meant by telling me of all the Indian things at the store.

"Can it be that they want me to dress Indian again? Are they ashamed of my school-dress?"

"Will they force me to spend my money for Indian things?"

I had already heard that two girls, who came back in the party with me, but who went to another village, had been whipped by the Governor and made to wear Indian clothes; that all their school clothes had been burned, and they were forced to do other terribly wicked things.

"Can it be that I shall have to suffer in the same way?"

"No, I think not," but as far as the Indian dress was concerned I could not help feeling that Indian clothes were much more comfortable than the kind I had on.

My mother did her washing at the water-hole much easier than I did in this tight dress.

My mother had no trouble in getting up and down the ladder, in her short dress.

She had no shoe-heels to catch on the rounds and nearly throw her off, as mine served me several times.

Everything hangs so loosely on her that she can stoop and climb and grind wheat and weave blankets and carry water and make jars and do everything lots easier than I can in this tight dress.

These thoughts all came to me as I stood looking at my mother putting on her shoes.

I made not a sign, however, to let them know what I was thinking about, but turning on my heel, said, " Well, come! Let us go to the store ! "

CHAPTER VII.

A TRIP TO THE STORE.

The burros were brought to the door, one for each of us.

My mother helped me mount, and was somewhat surprised to hear me exclaim, " Why, I cannot hold on. Where is the bridle ? "

"This is not a horse that you need a bridle. Don't you remember that we never bridle burros? You came up from the station all right," said my mother.

" Yes, I know, but I held fast to you."

" That is true," said she, " but sit with your feet hanging down so, and you will not fall off."

I laughed and did as she directed, but felt very insecure in my seat, not having any reins to help support me.

Then my mother gave me a sharp stick.

"Do you remember how to steer?" she asked.

"I do not."

"Jag his neck on the right side if you wish the burro to turn to the left, see?" and she started him off, thrusting the sharp stick into his shoulder.

Sure enough he did turn to the left so suddenly as nearly to throw me off backwards.

"How shall I stop him?"

Just then my mother called out "Whoa!" and followed it with "Chu, chu," in a loud whisper, which brought the animal to a dead halt, nearly sending me over his head.

Both my father and mother laughed at my awkwardness, and the merriment of the host of spectators who had gathered to see the school-girl mount a burro was unbounded.

We finally got started on our way over the rocks toward the road that led to the store.

As we jogged along, very little was said, but I kept up my usual amount of thinking.

I wondered what I should buy with my money, but determined not to buy anything foolish if I could help myself.

As we entered the store, the store-keeper was exceedingly cordial and gave my father a cigarette the first thing.

My mother went straight to the shawl-pile and, turning the bright-colored wraps over and over, selected one, saying : —

" Is n't that pretty ? "

" Beautiful ! Would you like to have it ? "

" I would indeed, but I have no money."

I bought the shawl and gave it to my mother, which pleased her much.

"Have you any washtubs?" I immediately asked the store-keeper.

"Plenty of them. Come this way!"

I followed him into an adjoining room.

Before directing my attention to the tubs, he asked: "Have you been away at school?"

"Yes, sir."

"Where?"

"At Carlisle," I was proud to answer.

"I thought so. Do you know I can tell a Carlisle girl whenever I see one?"

"How so?"

"Oh, I don't know. Carlisle is stamped on their very faces. I see it in every movement. They hold their heads up and speak English, and are not so timid that they cannot say what they want."

"I am glad to hear you speak well of my school, for I love Carlisle."

"Have you come home to stay?" he asked.

"I would like to go back again, but I do not believe my father and mother will let me."

"That is too bad."

"I do not believe they want to be unkind to me, but they think I know enough. I do not know half as much as I want to, though."

"I hope you can go back if you wish to, but if you have to stay you will not put on Indian clothes, will you?"

"No! Do you think I cannot appreciate what the great and good Government of the United States has done for me?

"Do you think I would be so ungrateful after the Government has spent so much time and money to educate me as not to use the knowledge I have ob-

tained? I see I cannot do much here, but I believe
I can keep myself right if I try. I can keep from
going back into Indian ways, if I am determined. I
don't believe that even the Governor could force
me back into the Indian dress. If he tried to, I
should run away. I believe the white people would
protect me if I should run to them."

"They would be glad to," said the store-keeper.

"The trouble with the girls is, they don't hold
out strong enough against these things. Some girls
who came home before I did wrote to me and said
they could not help it, they had to go back to the
Indian ways. I don't believe it. I mean to beat
out the Indian ways, if such a thing is possible, and
I believe it *is* possible."

"I am glad to hear you talk so earnestly. To
help you, I will sell you what you want cheaper than
I usually sell."

"Thank you. Oh, there are the tubs. I will take one of the medium sized ones."

He selected one which suited.

"And now a washboard."

"This one?" he asked.

"Yes, thank you. Have you flat-irons?"

"How many?"

"Three, please."

These were put to one side with the rest of the things.

"I see you have bedsteads. I would like one of the single cots, please."

"Anything else?" asked the store-keeper. I could see that he wondered at my having so much money.

"Yes, sir. I want a mattress to fit the bed."

"Of course. And do you not want some dishes and a table? Here is a small table for a dollar."

I bought it and a dish-pan and some knives and forks, two chairs, some sugar and coffee and tea and other things to eat.

I paid for each article as I bought it, and when done had one dollar and a half left, with which I purchased my father a whole suit of clothes, including the white man's hat.

Every cent of my money was gone, and I had not bought a bead or a piece of buckskin for myself, and I was happy.

I was sorry to spend *all* my money, but it was better for me to spend it all in that way than to save some to spend afterwards in a way that I should not wish to.

My father and mother soon had the things tied on the burros.

They put all the largest things on my burro, and I rode home with my mother.

By the time the little animal had the bedstead, the tub, the table and chairs tied on him, he looked funny enough.

The load was not heavy, but bulky.

I have often seen burros with piles of wood on their backs so immense that all one could see of the tiny creatures were their ears and tails and feet.

It was night before we got home, and by the time we had all the things carried up the ladder, had eaten our suppers, and made the beds, we were tired enough to sleep well.

My father helped me put the new bedstead together.

I offered it to my mother, but of course she preferred the floor, never having slept in any other place.

That night I enjoyed the first comfortable sleep since leaving my room at Carlisle.

BURROS LOADED WITH WOOD

CHAPTER VIII.

ANNIE'S FEARS.

ABOUT ten o'clock next morning I heard some
one coming up the ladder, and, going to see who it
was, found my friend Annie G., who returned from
Carlisle at the same time I did, but who went on to
another village where she lived.

"Why, Annie, is that you?" I cried. "I am so
glad to see you."

"Are you?" she replied looking up pleasantly,
but on reaching the top she threw her arms around
my neck and sobbed as though her heart would
break.

"What *is* the matter?" I inquired anxiously.

"Nothing, only I have been almost wild to see you. I don't like it here at all. Oh, Stiya, let us go back to Carlisle, quick."

"Don't let us talk about that now! Come into the house, my friend. It was good of you to come to see me."

My mother had gone for water, and my father too was out, so we had the house to ourselves, for which I was very glad.

I noticed Annie looking at the chairs rather curiously, and through her tears she exclaimed, "Why, Stiya, where did you get these nice chairs?"

"I bought them."

"I wish *we* had some. I do get so tired sitting on little blocks of wood and on the floor."

"So did I, and that is the reason I bought chairs." Then I proudly showed her all the things I had purchased the day before.

" Where did you get so much money, Stiya ? "

" I saved the money earned in the country when I was at Carlisle. Did n't you have any money when you came back ? "

" I had some when I started, but I spent it all for candy, fruit and nuts, and other things which the news-boy on the cars had for sale. Do you remember him ? Did n't we have a jolly good time coming out ? "

" A good time, to be sure, but it made me sick to see the boys and girls throwing their money away for candy. I did n't spend twenty-five cents. How much did you spend ? "

" Every cent of ten dollars."

" Ten dollars ! Why, Annie ! You wish you had the money now, don't you ? "

" I guess I do, but I never thought I would need it for such things as these. I forgot that my people were poor."

" Did n't you have more than ten dollars ? "

" No. You remember my father would not let me go out into the country to work. He said he did not want me to be a slave. I could work enough at home, he said."

" Why, I think the few months they give us at Carlisle in country homes is the very best thing for us, don't you? I can never forget my splendid home in the country. How Mrs. R. used to talk to me about saving my money and taking care of my clothes! How kind she was to me, and patient! She taught me to bake and cook, and I learned English so fast there that I could hardly believe my own ears. To tell the truth, I used to like to hear myself talk, it was so new and strange and nice. I would not take a great deal for what I learned in the country."

" Our people don't know what is really good for us, do they? " said Annie in distress.

" Not always, I think."

" But we have to obey our parents."

" Certainly! It is best to obey our fathers and
mothers, but, Annie, I think we know so much more
than they do now that if we are kind to them we
ought at the same time to do what we know is right,
even if it is contrary to what they wish. Don't you
think so? I am sure they will let us do the right
if they see we are really in earnest."

" No," said Annie, her eyes filling again with
tears, " I am afraid they will not. My mother is
beginning already to talk about my putting on
the Indian dress. Everybody in the village makes
fun of me, too; " and here Annie broke out into
another uncontrollable fit of crying.

" Well, don't cry, Annie dear. I'll tell you what
to do. I have thought it all over. How I have
thought since I came home! I have been sad and

angry, and disheartened and homesick, all at once,
determined one minute, and weak the next. I
thought when I first came I could not stay over
night in such a place. But I have gotten over that
already. We must not be cowards. When your
mother talks to you about Indian clothes, begin to
tell the family something nice about the East or
something you have learned."

" But they won't listen to me."

" Don't say to them, I WILL NOT put on Indian
dress. That makes them try all the more to have
you do so. Keep quiet about the Indian dress, and
every time you get a chance to do a kind thing for
any of the family, do so, and ask your mother to
let you bake some bread, or cook something."

" I did bake once, but I cannot make good
bread out of this Indian flour. And I am not used
to these little Indian ovens, and my bread was all

burned and sour and hard. I was heartily ashamed
of it, and they laughed at it, too."

"Try a cake, then, that is not so hard to bake."

"We have no butter, no eggs, no sugar."

"Oh, I forgot that. At any rate," said I deter-
minedly, "there is a way. There must be a way.
It will come all right if we don't get discouraged.
We must not give up. I don't care how strong the
pressure is, I shall not put on Indian dress. If my
mother whips me, I shall not do it. If she shuts
me up in a room and starves me, I shall not do it.
If the Governor says he will kill me, I shall not do
it. If everybody in the village points a finger of
scorn at me and laughs at me and calls me bad
names, I shall not do it. I *am not going to put on
Indian dress*, do you hear?"

"Oh, Stiya, do you think it is possible to be so
brave?" said Annie, throwing herself on her knees

and burying her face in my lap. "You may be right, but I want to get away from it all. I want to go back again to school, where we will see none of this, and not have to stand this persecution."

"It is when we are afraid and want to run away that they see weakness in our faces, and that is the time they always take to talk about these Indian · ways," said I, while stroking the distressed girl's hair.

Here a cry was heard outside. "What is that?" said Annie in a whisper, as she suddenly lifted her head from my lap.

CHAPTER IX.

THE VILLAGE CRIER.

WE went to the door and listened.

On a housetop near stood an old man, the crier of the village, calling at the top of his voice : —

"A dance ! A dance ! This afternoon, in so-and-so's house ! Everybody come ! The Governor orders ! "

He repeated the words over and over again, each time louder than the time before, until one would think his throat would burst.

"One of those disgraceful dances," I said, turning to Annie. "I thought they had given them up in our two villages."

"That is what Belle wrote me before we started home, but since this new Governor was elected, she said things have been going backward."

"I had not heard it."

"Yes," continued Annie, "Belle wrote that this Governor has around him a lot of old-time officers who believe in the old Indian ways, and the people are again talking about the dances."

"I suppose, then, this is the first dance of the season. Is n't it too bad that the Indians who have gotten ahead somewhat have to follow such a leader as this Governor, who seems to be trying to lead them back where they were in the first place?"

"It certainly is a shame, and I think something ought to be done to prevent it," said Annie.

"May be there will be some time. Have you *seen* Belle, yet?" I asked.

"No, she left for the Albuquerque school before

we arrived. She went away from here as soon as
she could, and I wish *we* were out of this, too, don't
you? Just listen to that horrid man! Did you
ever go to a dance, Stiya?"

" Not this kind."

" Neither did I, because before we went to Carlisle we were too little. But I have heard they are
forcing all the girls who came back this summer to
go."

" That is dreadful! Although we have not been
to a dance, we have heard our older girl friends tell
about them, and know nearly as well what they do
as if we had been there ourselves, don't we ?"

" I think we do, and my heart shudders now at
the terrible things I have heard. At one time I did
not think they were terrible. I can remember crying to go with my mother to these very dances, but
now I should be ashamed to be seen in such a
place."

"Do they really do such fearful things?"

"Too terrible for you and me to talk about; too bad to even *think* about. Let us go in the house, Stiya. I hate to listen to that man calling the people to go to such a place."

Just as we were about to turn to go inside, my mother came hurrying up the ladder all out of breath and carrying a bundle.

"Come, my daughter," she said. "Get ready! We must go!"

"Go where? Mother, this is Annie G., who came back with me from Carlisle. She lives in Pa-*hwa*-ke village, you know."

She looked at Annie, shook hands, and asked whose daughter she was.

"My mother's name is Ke-ma-*net*-sa," replied Annie modestly.

"Se! Se!" my mother exclaimed. "Ke-ma-

net-sa ! We used to be girls together," she continued, while stroking Annie's arm.

The crier again sounded his great voice through
the air : " A dance ! A dance ! Everybody come !
The Governor orders ! "

" There ! " she said with a sudden turn. " Get
ready ! We must hurry."

My heart sank within me. " Mother," I said
plaintively, " I do not want to go to that dance."

" Don't be crazy," she replied. " You must go.
Here are your cousin's dress and leggings. I
brought them for you. Put them on quickly and
let us go ! You can't go to a dance in that dress !
They would not let you in," she added with a hard
smile. " And I want to cut your hair off, too."

Without a word Annie got up and left. I heard
her go down the ladder, and the sound of her shoe-
heels on the rocks below came back in faint echoes

as my mother and I sat there in silence, each waiting for the other to speak.

"Come!" she finally said. "Are you not going to put on that dress?"

"Mother, you are not going to make me put it on if I don't want to, are you?" said I, almost crying.

"The Governor says you must go to the dance."

"What right has the Governor to say I must go?"

"My daughter, we have to obey the Governor."

"That is a very bad dance, and I don't want to go."

"It isn't bad," my mother replied, indignantly. "It is the Indian way. It is the way we have always been used to. You are Indian, if you *have* been off to school, learning the ways of the white folks. They can't make you anything but Indian after all."

" Yes, I am Indian, mother. But I have learned better ways, and I do not have to do the Indian ways any more if I don't want to, do I ? "

" We will see about that," and as she spoke she flew down the ladder and out of sight.

CHAPTER X.

THE GOVERNOR.

I was now alone.

"What *shall* I do? What shall I *do?*" I murmured as I paced back and forth in the little room.

"Where has my mother gone? Perhaps for my father. Now is my time. Shall I run away?"

I went to the door. There were men, women, and children to be seen everywhere, on the house-tops and hurrying from house to house on the rocks below. No! I could not run away. I would be followed and caught so easily. Ought I to run away if I could?

Never! That would not be "standing by a purpose true," as our Superintendent used to say we
must when in a hard place. Here was my first real
hard place since coming home. Here was a chance
for me to show what I was made of.

"But, see! Who is that making such swift
strides in this direction?"

"My father, my mother, and the Governor, as
sure as I am alive."

My heart thumped as I had never felt it before.
I turned and went quickly into the house.

Picking up an apron I had started to make just
before my friend Annie arrived in the morning, I
sat in apparent composure, sewing when the party
entered.

"The Governor!" announced my father as they
crossed the threshold.

I arose with as much dignity and coolness as the

circumstances would allow, and shook the Governor's hand.

His keen black eye searched me through and through as I stood before him. Having done nothing to be ashamed of, I looked him fairly and squarely in the face.

" The dance! " said my father, still out of breath, not having recovered from his fast walking.

" I understand there is to be one," said I, again picking up my apron to sew.

" Are you ready ? " he asked.

" I thought I would not go this afternoon, father."

" Why not ? " asked he excitedly.

" I have this apron to finish, and then I want to make you a shirt, father, when I get this done."

Looking up quickly, I saw the Governor cast a glance of ridicule at my father.

I felt indignant and hurt. If there is anything that arouses the ire of an Indian, — man or woman, boy or girl, savage or civilized, — it is to be made fun of.

I could not stand it even from a Governor, hence I arose, took my hat from the nail, picked up my parasol, and started for the door.

" Where are you going ? " asked my mother, stepping between me and the door.

" Only for a little walk. I will be back soon."

" You can't go for a walk," said my father. " The Governor is here to see you."

" I have come to see you about the dance," responded the Governor.

" You may as well make up your mind to go," said my mother, " for if you don't go of your own free will we will take you by force."

I felt every muscle and nerve in me twinge.

Cry?

I could not.

"Is this the way my liberty is to be taken from me? Having been educated out of and away from this superstition, am I still to be a slave to it? Must I submit?"

I said not a word, but stood stone still. If my brown face is capable of looking pale, it must have been pale at that moment.

Rigid, with eyes fastened on the Governor and with lips tightly compressed, I stood before them.

"Come," said my mother finally. "Your father and the Governor will go out while you put on your cousin's dress."

"Mother," said I as tenderly as my voice would allow, but in low and measured tones, "I want to be good to you because you are my mother, but I shall not put on that dress."

"Stop such crazy talk," said my father, now excited to the highest pitch; at the same time he seized me by the shoulders and shook me angrily.

"My father!" I cried, "will you be so cruel to your own daughter? O father dear, do help me!" I implored, throwing my arms around his neck and sobbing bitterly.

My mother then began to cry. She said I was not a dutiful daughter.

I wanted to bring disgrace upon the family and have the whole village laughing at us. She said Carlisle school had done me no good. I had come back to disobey my parents. I had always obeyed before I went away to that school.

"I did not want you to go, and now I am sorry I let you go," she went on. "The white folks have taught you to disobey." She cried and talked at such a rate, and with voice so monotonous and

pitched so high, that men, women, and children outside began to gather around the foot of the ladder
to see what was the matter.

I cried as hard as she, but said nothing. As my
father did not push me from him, I felt that he was
weakening in my favor, and as his great breast
heaved with excitement, I could but take courage in
the thought that there was power in him to help me.

The Governor arose, and with insolent coolness
took my hands and tried to loosen my hold upon my
father's neck.

"Go away!" I screamed, shuddering at his touch.

"Let her alone," said my father, pushing the
Governor back, and from that moment I loved my
father as I never had before.

"What do you mean?" asked the Governor.

"I mean that she is my child and you shall not
force her to do what she does not want to do."

"What! Do you defy me openly like this?
Do you disobey the Governor? Am I not the
ruler?" said he, striking himself upon the breast,
and taking me again by the arm he tried to separate
me from my father, saying, "You shall go to the
dance!"

I felt now that my father would protect me.

Wrenching myself from the Governor's grasp I
stood erect, and looking him in the eye said boldly,
"I shall not go to the dance."

My mother flew to my side, and tearing my hat
from my head threw it into the corner, and taking
me by my left arm motioned the Governor to take
the other. He did so, and the two dragged me to
the top of the ladder.

"If you will not put on your cousin's dress you
shall go in this dress," said my mother as she pulled
and I resisted.

" Woman ! " cried my father, " what are you doing ? " and springing for mother he caught her
around the waist, lifted her and gave her a forcible
shove through the door.

He went in after her, shut the door, and I could
hear him " reading law " to her as the white folks
would say, while she moaned and talked back in
such manner as is possible for an uncivilized Indian
woman only under proper conditions.

I was left alone outside with the Governor, but
was no longer afraid. I did not attempt to withdraw from his hold until my father stepped to the
door after the fracas within had somewhat subsided,
and said : —

" Come here, my daughter ! "

Then I tried to move, but could not.

" Come here ! " said my father again.

" I cannot," said I, looking anxiously toward the
door.

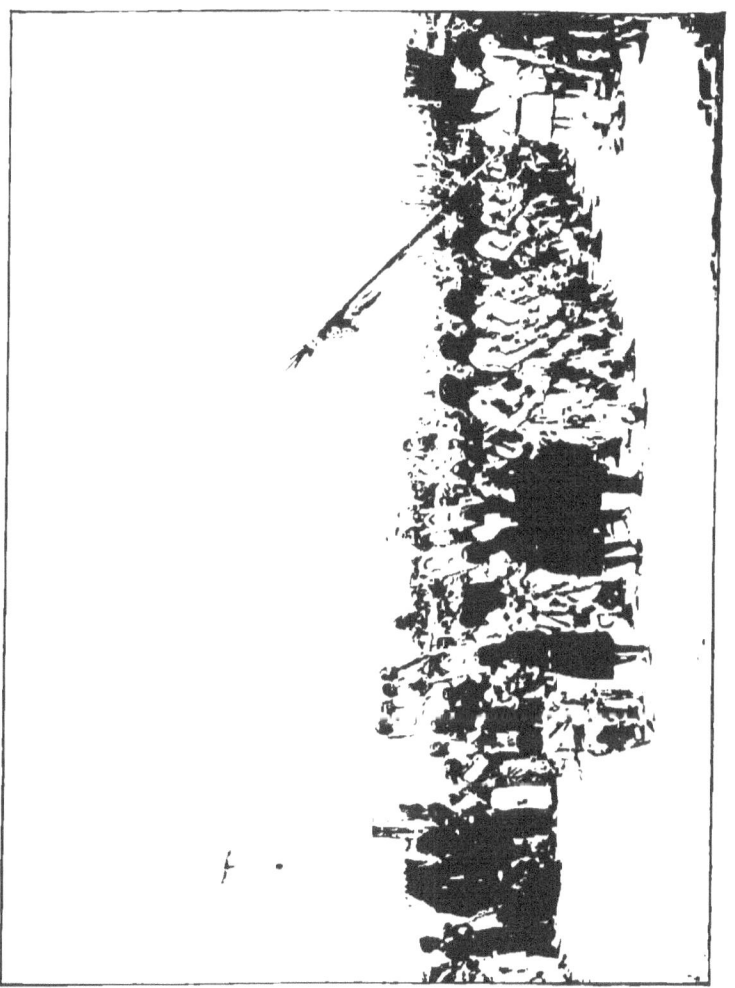

SUN-DANCE AT CATHOLIC MISSION

The Governor was angry enough to send me headlong over the edge of the roof, had he dared, but as I did not go to my father, both he and my mother appeared on the scene, and I could see that my mother was a changed woman.

She stepped up to the Governor and said, " My daughter will go with me into the house."

" To put on the Indian dress ? " he inquired as he released my arm.

" No," she said. " My daughter does not want to go to the dance, and she need not."

I was dumbfounded.

My father and mother, too, on my side ? What could it all mean ? And then the old saying learned at Carlisle, " WHERE THERE IS A WILL THERE IS A WAY," came into my head.

I had used my WILL, and the WAY had come.

My father's will and my mother's will had come to help my will to do what was right.

The Governor's will was not bent, however, in the direction of right.

My father prevented him from following us, and he had nothing to do but go back to his home. As he passed down the ladder I could hear him grumbling to himself and to the people below.

" They shall suffer for this ! Three of my people have disobeyed me. I am the Governor."

" Our Governor must be obeyed," shouted several in the crowd.

" To the dance ! To the dance !" I could hear him crying in the distance. " After the dance I will call my officers. We will have a meeting, and settle whether that Carlisle girl and her people shall rule this village or the Governor whom the people elect."

CHAPTER XI.

EVIL FOREBODINGS.

THE dance was over, and I had not gone !

But that night as I lay upon my pillow, the shuffling and talking of Indians, passing on their way home from the disgraceful gathering, filled me with unspeakable discomfort.

By taking a strong stand I felt that I had done a good thing, not only for myself, but for my father and mother.

I felt it to be of the greatest importance for us Carlisle girls to take such stands when we knew that we were in the right.

We should do the right even if it hurts badly to do it.

From the experience of the afternoon I realized as never before how much my father and mother really loved me, and I determined stronger than ever to help them in every possible way; still, the feeling that calamity was about to befall us as a family, by reason of my having taken a stand for the right, very much disturbed me.

As I lay there, I went over the conversation of the afternoon.

I could see again the anxious look upon my father's face as he said, " The Governor will make it hard for us."

" Yes," my mother had answered tremblingly, while looking toward me, " and you have brought this trouble upon us."

How I was weighed down at that moment with the tremendous responsibility of having led my father to disobey the Governor !

I had thrown it off, however, and said lightly, " I
don't believe we will have any great trouble."

" The Governor is a hard man," said my father,
shaking his head.

" We are not afraid of him, are we ? " said I.

" We are right. I KNOW we are right," I continued. " These dances are not good for our people.
Our white friends, who know what we need better
than we know ourselves, advise us to give up all our
superstitious dances, and especially this low-down
kind that is going on this afternoon. Somebody
must begin to stay away from them. Whoever is
the first to oppose them will have to stand the
sneers of the whole village. I have made the beginning in this village, and oh my father, my mother,
you stood so bravely by me to-day ; can you not always thus stand by me? We are strong if we stand
together. No matter what comes, let us not give up
the RIGHT ! "

Every word I had said and the anxious look of distress and fear which my mother wore, all came vividly to my mind, as I lay on my little cot at that midnight hour.

Then there were steps upon the ladder.

My father and mother were both asleep, so I went quietly to the door to see who was coming, and there in the dim moonlight stood my friend Annie, again.

"Why, Annie, where *did* you come from at this hour of the night; and in Indian clothes, too? Annie! Annie! What does this mean?" I whispered.

"My mother took my school-clothes from me, and left me nothing else to put on," she explained.

"And you could not help yourself?"

"Could not do a thing, and that is not the worst of it, either," said Annie.

" You have n't been to the dance? "

" Yes, I have. My father and mother and sister, all three, dragged me to the very door, and pushed me in."

" Horrors ! " I exclaimed, throwing up my hands. " Where are they now? "

" They went home, but allowed me to stay with my aunt over night. She was asleep, and I slipped over here to tell you what I heard about you."

" Now, what dreadful thing ? "

" They are going publicly to whip you and your father and mother."

" They would not dare do such a thing, Annie; it cannot be true ! The officers have had no meeting since this afternoon, to come to any such decision."

" They held a meeting this evening while the dance was going on, and before it was over the

Governor came and told us what was to be done. Can't you run away, Stiya, dear? It will break my heart for you to be whipped. Let us start now! If we walk all night, we will be out of their reach in the morning, and then by to-morrow night we will be at the Albuquerque school. Come! let us go! won't you? I would rather starve on the way than stay here!"

"What?" said I, "and leave my father and mother, on whom I have brought this trouble? No indeed!"

"Then I will just give up and do everything the Indian way."

"Don't, Annie, don't talk so, not even in fun!"

"Well, there is no use in trying."

"Oh, yes, there is."

"Everything and everybody are against us."

"It seems so; but we must not give up yet. Let

us try a hundred ways before we allow ourselves to be discouraged!"

"Grace and Mary and Virginia and Kate and Josie were all at the dance, and all in Indian dress. All said they were made to go."

"What *will* the teachers at Carlisle think when they hear this?"

"They will be grieved, of course, but they don't know how hard it is to stand for the right, out here, do they?" said Annie.

"It isn't so hard that we cannot come out best, do you think?" I asked.

"I have been defeated, at any rate, and so will you be," whispered Annie as she glided down the ladder, and said "Good-night," in the same breath.

CHAPTER XII.

PERSECUTION.

DEFEATED ? How the word rang in my ears as I turned back into the house!

Defeated ? For an hour I believe I lay pondering over the dreadful situation as pictured by my friend Annie, and I made plan after plan to evade what seemed sure to come, on the morrow.

Defeated ? The word in connection with Annie's whispered prophecy, "I have been defeated, and so will you be," threw me into a nightmare of despair.

How slowly the morning dawned! Yet, how I wished it would never come!

The awfulness of the day that followed can never be described.

I will not harrow the feelings of those interested in my story by attempting a detailed picture of the terrible scene.

Enough to say that my father, mother, and I were stripped of our clothing, bound and dragged through the narrow passageways of the old Pueblo, and on bare backs lashed, until bleeding and sore we were taken to the Governor's lock-up, thrust into the damp and dingy hole, there to spend hours of suffering and hunger.

My father received forty stripes, but with true Indian stoicism he never winced.

My mother's sentence was twenty-five, and at every blow, poor soul, she screamed frantically, while I attempted, in the twenty which were my portion, to imitate the bravery of my father.

In the midst of the fearful agony and excitement,
thoughts of dear Carlisle came to me, — my duties
in the school-room, in the dining-hall, in the
laundry, in the cooking-class, in the sewing-room, in
the quarters, — the whole beautiful picture of sweet
content on the faces of the boys and girls, as they
went their daily rounds, loomed up before me and
gave me courage. I even remembered how at times
I had been a little tired, and thought the work and
studies harder than they ought to be, and how then
for a few moments I would wish for home and
friends, for father and mother, and for the bright
New Mexico sun. But I never dreamed that when
I did come home I would experience such a trial as
this.

" What have I done to merit it ? "

" I have stood for the RIGHT, that is all."

" This is what a Carlisle school-girl must endure,

is it, if she wishes to follow the RIGHT ? " said I to myself.

" But I CAN endure it, yes, and I WILL endure it. Strike me again ; hit harder, you cruel man ! " I said to the brute of an officer, who seemed already to be straining every muscle to make me cringe, and then holding my breath and clinching my teeth, I stood ready for the blow that followed.

I could have endured twice the pain.

I was RIGHT.

I KNEW I was right, and that made me strong.

I must have been a surprise to all the lookers-on, for they stared at me so, and especially so to Annie, whose tearful eyes and anxious face I saw more than once peering through the crowd.

After all was over, and the door of the jail into which we were thrust was locked, I, with my mother, fell into a dead swoon.

How long we lay in the presence of my horror-stricken father I know not, and he does not seem able to tell.

There we lay, dead, as my father thought.

An Indian knows not the difference between a faint and death.

Many an Indian in camp, no doubt, has been buried alive, for as soon as unconscious, a blanket is thrown over the face, and the body hurried off for burial; especially is this so if the person is one of no great importance in the tribe.

I came to consciousness first, and saw my father in the dim light standing with his back to us, but staring backward at us with awe-stricken and ghastly expression.

"Father," I cried, "come! I am all right."

He came and stood near.

Having been taught while at school how to bring

a person out of a faint, I caught up a water-jar,
which had fortunately been left by mistake in the
room and which contained a few drops of stale
water, and threw its contents into my mother's face,
which brought her almost immediately to consciousness, greatly to my father's astonishment and relief.

I can never forget his look when he fully realized
that my mother was alive once more, and how proud
his gaze as he said : —

"My daughter, you are a wonderful girl. You
are a brave girl. It made me strong when I was
being whipped by that dog to see you so heroically
stand the dreaded blows upon *your* back. I believe
now more than ever that you are right. I believe
you have with you the white man's God. I intend
more than ever to follow you. I am your father
and should be able to lead you, but the old Indian
way is not good. I don't know the white man's

way. Can I learn it? I *will* learn it. THEY can't
make me do what you don't want me to," said he
earnestly, proudly straightening himself in defiance
of the noisy crowd outside, while tears now for the
first time stood in his great, strong, loving eyes, as
they rested upon me.

CHAPTER XIII.

HOME AGAIN.

AFTER forty-eight hours of untold discomfort in
the dingy lock-up our clothing was thrown to us,
and we were allowed to go home.

On the way, I asked my father, "Are you sorry
you did not go to the dance?"

"I never was more proud in my life," he answered, with head aloft and firm, dignified tread.
"I am proud that you are my daughter. I am proud
of your mother. I am proud that I have a mind of
my own. Let them whip us again! We are on the
right road! I am not afraid! I have been thinking about this road a long time. I knew I should

have a hard time when I made the start. You are
the cause of it, but I am glad. I shall hold on, and
you will help me. We will all go along together.
We will have other very hard things to bear. They
will call me ' old woman,' " he continued motioning
toward the Indians gazing out of the doors and
windows of the old Pueblo houses. " They will say
I am helping the Government and fighting against
my own people, but they will see by and by that we
are right. They will soon see that we are better
off than they are. I know what I am about. Let
them talk! Let them laugh! I have my senses. I
am not ashamed."

I never heard my father talk so fast or so earnestly.

He reminded me of men in council.

Women and girls don't go to Indian councils as a
rule, but I had often stopped outside the council-

room to listen, or look at them through the window.
Sometimes two or three men would speak at once
about this thing or that, rolling out one long sentence after another, going on and on and on in
the same tone of voice as though every word were
understood, when in fact not many words were heard.
That mattered not, on and on and on they sped,
like talking machines wound up, until I thought
they never *could* stop. But my father was more
earnest than they.

I remember when at school we girls used to talk
about the customs of our people, and one day I was
telling a company of my friends about the way the
Pueblos held their meetings and the way the men
sit and talk.

"You say, 'sit and talk!' Don't your chiefs stand
up, when they speak to the people?" asked Vinnie,
a Pawnee.

"Chiefs! We do not have chiefs. We have a Governor elected every year, and he appoints his officers to help him."

"And when they hold meetings, the men do not stand up to speak?" asked one of the girls.

"Sometimes they do,". I said, "but often the longest and loudest talkers keep seated all the while they are speaking. I remember one man in particular, who used to sit on the floor in the corner, and spin an interminable number of words even about a very small subject."

But to go back to my home story.

My father felt in the talking mood as he walked home from the lock-up, and even after we reached our little room he kept on saying that he meant to do this thing and that, and the Governor could not scare him out of doing what he thought was right. "I intend to follow you, my daughter!"

My mother was exhausted and nearly sick by the time she reached home.

I, too, was tired and hungry, but I had learned from a few little experiences the truth of what we were sometimes told at Carlisle, if one has trouble or is only a little sick, it is often better to *work* it off than to sit down, hang the head, and brood over it. Brooding makes trouble grow bigger, and sickness grow worse; so I flew around as though nothing unusual had happened, and as though I were not tired.

The table bought the day I went to the store had never been used. My father and mother seemed to prefer eating in the same old way from the dishes placed on the floor, and I never urged a change. But now if I prepared the supper, the table must come into use.

We would begin now to live differently. Our

suffering had put the old life away from us, and we would begin a new one.

I found the things in the room very much as we had left them. There was flour in the sack, and baking powder in a box.

Instead of the Mexican tortilla that my mother and all the Pueblo women know so well how to make, I made Carlisle biscuit, and baked them in a pan covered over with hot ashes.

Then I made a frizzle out of the dried mutton I took from the line, using water instead of milk, which, with tea, made up our supper.

I spread the table with two newspapers I happened to have in my trunk, and set the things on as tastefully as it was possible to do under the circumstances, and then drew up the chairs and asked my father and mother to come and eat what they had been so curiously watching me prepare.

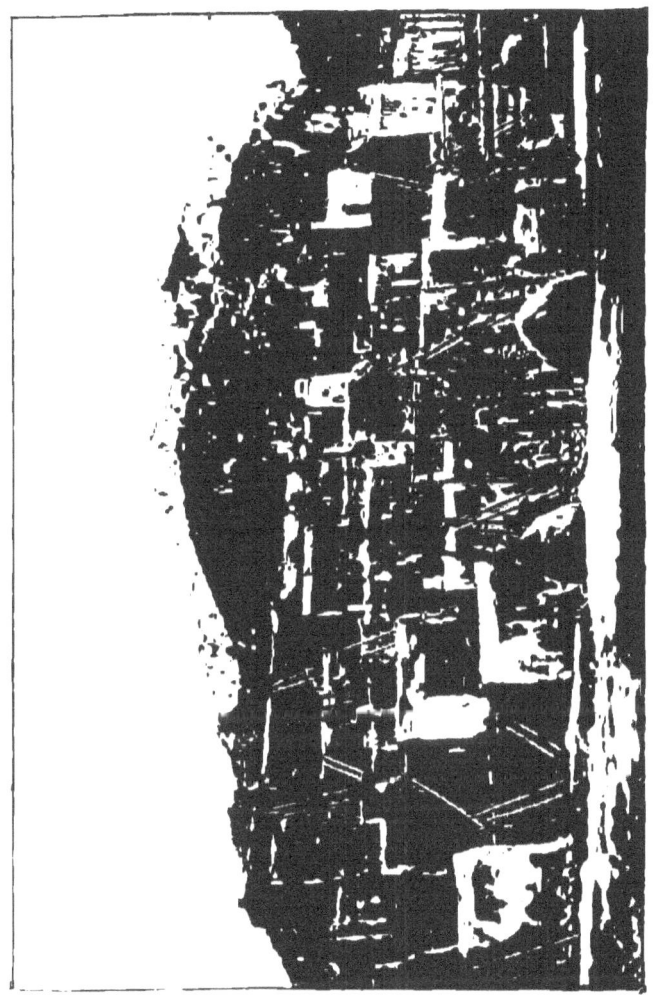

PUEBLO VILLAGE

" This is nice," said my father. " We will never eat from the floor again, will we ? " asked he of my mother.

She did not say much. I could see that she felt miserable, and I advised her to lie down.

She did so after I had made her bed on the floor, and was soon fast asleep from exhaustion, while my father and I continued to eat and talk.

We talked of everything except that which was uppermost in our minds, from the effects of which we both were suffering at the time.

" Father," I said, " how long do you think we will have to live in this little room. I wish we had a larger house."

" We shall have a larger house. We might have had one long ago if I had paid more attention to work and not wasted so much time dancing. I am going to Seama to live. I like the people there. Don't you ? "

"You mean where Miss S—— teaches school?"
I asked.

"Yes, I think that is the white lady's name. She
has a good school, and the children of the village
all go to her school, and she teaches them good
things. That village is ahead of all the Indian villages around, and I believe it is on account of the
school. I want to live in a place where the people
think more about school than foolish things. We
will go to Seama to live, may we daughter?"

"I would be glad to go anywhere to get out of
this thousand - year - old place, — this Pueblo where
there are so many who want to go in the old Indian
way; but, father, how are we to live in Seama, without a house to live in, and no money to buy one
with?"

"I will tell you," said he with a smile.

CHAPTER XIV.

DIFFICULTIES OVERCOME.

I KNEW there would be a way to get the new
house if father once made up his mind. With a
face the picture of determination he arose from the
table, went out and down the ladder as I thought to
look after the burros, they having had no attention
since we were in the lock-up. Still, as a general
thing, a burro thrives better the less attention he
gets, so we did not feel anxious about them.

My mother slept the sleep of one exhausted, and
I sat and mused a moment or two after my father
left, but the words of my farm-mother, away in the
East, came to me as clearly as if I had heard the

dear lady say, " Come! this will not do," the very
thing she used to say to her own children, as well
as myself, when we sat wasting time and doing
nothing.

I arose quickly, cleared off the table, carefully
folded the newspapers, put them back in my trunk
for next time, and thought : —

" Dear, oh, dear ! What shall I do for a table-
cloth when they are gone ? "

Then I put some water in a boiler over the fire to
heat, for now was my chance to wash that pile of
clay plates, iron pans, pots, tin spoons, cups, and
other eating utensils stacked away in the corner on
the floor.

One would naturally suppose that using the same
dishes day after day without proper washing would
cause a filthy accumulation of dried food around
the edges and in the corners and crevices.

The fact is, the ordinary Pueblo family do not
have food in such superabundance and variety that
they can afford to leave much sticking around the
edges; but should a vestige of anything "smella-
ble" be accidentally overlooked, the family dog
visits the corner into which the dishes are shoved,
and "does up the work."

I had seen our dogs do so more than once.

But though there was not a great deal of hard,
dry waste on the pans and pots and dishes, I knew
how unclean they must be, and while my mother
slept was the chance for me to wash them.

But where should I get a dish-cloth?

Not a rag about that I could use for that purpose.

I could not do as the girls at schools said their
mammas did, wipe out the dishes with dry prairie
grass, for not a blade of grass grew upon the rocks
on which our village was built.

And they said, too, that when their mammas preferred a rag to grass they tore off a piece of their skirts, the garment next the body being the one used to supply the family with rags and strings.

No, I could not do that, but what? That was the question?

"I know," said I to myself, a happy thought striking me. "There is that old calico dress in my trunk."

I was half angry with my school-mother as I stood by her side at Carlisle, while she was packing my trunk and filling in the chinks with old garments that I thought were of no use, but they were clean, and had my name on, and now I know in the kindness of her heart she thought they might be of some use to me away out here, and she put them in instead of throwing them away.

How I did thank her as I took the old dress out

of my trunk and tore it up into cloths, one for a towel to dry the dishes, and one to wash them with !

As I sat by the fireplace on the floor, for I did not want to blacken my table, I could not help thinking how shocked my farm-mother would be if she saw me that minute washing dishes on the floor with a piece of calico dress, and drying them with another piece, when she had taught me to keep the dish-cloth in a certain place, and it must be so clean, and the dish towels were kept as white as snow all the time.

" Well," I said to myself, " this is the very best I can do just now. If I do the very best I can all the time, I don't care what any one says. I will keep these calico rags clean at least, if they are *not* white."

" The very first chance I get, and the first money I get, I shall buy towels."

And I went on talking to myself as I worked : —

" If the girls at Carlisle would buy useful things they might need when they go home, instead of spending their money for ribbons and rings and fine shoes, and other things they are so often advised not to buy, how much more sensible it would be."

I wished, too, as I worked there on the floor that I were a Carlisle girl again, getting ready to come home. I would lay in a stock of towels, and a dish-cloth or two, after this bitter experience.

In the midst of my reveries my mother awoke. Poor woman ! She looked so sick and tired.

" Where is your father ? " she asked, looking around in a bewildered way.

" He went out some time ago, and I don't see why he does n't come back," I replied anxiously.

CHAPTER XV.

TRUE COURAGE.

My mother arose, and went to the door.

" I hear nothing and see nothing of him," she said. " Why does n't he come back? "

Going also to the door, I laid my arm gently over her shoulder, while we both stood peering out into the night.

" Do you think the Governor has seized your father? " sobbed my mother, as she turned and again sought her bed, almost overcome with weakness.

" Oh, no, mother. I can't think so. The Governor has had enough of us. Father has stepped into some house, and is talking longer than he thinks. He will be here soon," I said, trying to calm her fears.

"There is no house for him to go into. Nobody will talk to us any more. They would be afraid to speak to us. Everything goes wrong. I shall be afraid every day, now," she sighed. "You make us trouble all the time, just as the white folks always have done."

"Don't mother! Don't talk so! You are not well. When you get better, everything will be all right. Let me make you some tea! You did n't eat much supper," said I, giving the fire a poke.

"What are you doing there," she asked, observing for the first time the clean dishes not yet stacked away.

"Oh, I only washed the dishes, that is all."

"They were clean enough before," she muttered, turning her back, while I, disheartened and anxious, said not another word ; and before the tea was done she had fallen asleep.

I then placed the dishes away in the corner, and spread over them the piece of cloth I had used in drying them, determined that no dog should visit that corner as long as I was around.

Then I set the table back, spread my father's bed upon the floor, and went to the door again to listen.

" It must be all of eleven o'clock. Why does n't he come ? "

" What if I never see him again ? " I whispered, fairly frightened at the thought. " The Governor was very angry with him because he did not wince when the heavy blows were laid across his back. Has he caught him out alone ? Have they quarreled ? Has he been shoved off this terrible rock into one of the great crevices, 400 feet deep ? Does my father lie there in the darkness, dead ? "

I could not allow myself to think another moment in that strain, and turned back into the room. After putting on a stick or two of wood, I went to my trunk and took out all my INDIAN HELPERS, which I had kept so carefully between two pasteboard box covers. At school, every week when done reading the little paper I put it in my trunk.

"I *thought* I would be glad to have you in my home," said I, talking to them as though they were a person. "And now I *am* glad."

I really believe I kissed the papers, I was so pleased to have them at that lonely hour of the night. I sat down by the fire, and for an hour lost myself reading over what we had done at Carlisle in years gone by.

But after an hour had passed thus I felt an uncontrollable uneasiness creeping over me.

"Why don't my father come?"

Again I went to the door. Yes, out to the ladder's top.

A full hour must have passed, and yet no sound of his footstep. Should I go in search of him?

I went back for my coat, but when in the room my better judgment said : —

"Foolish girl! go to bed!"

I did so, but could not sleep.

Hour after hour passed, and finally the morning began to dawn.

"Oh, father, father; where are you?" I was saying, when he entered the door.

I sprang to my feet and rushed into his arms, crying, "Where have you been? I have not slept a wink, fearing that harm had come to you; and mother, too, has been anxious. Why, how black your face is, and your hands! Father, dear, what have you been doing?"

His eyes fairly glistened with pleasure as he answered, "Shoveling coal."

I could scarcely believe my ears.

"Shoveling coal? Why, father, where is there any coal around here to shovel? Who has coal to shovel?" I asked.

"The man at the station," he replied.

"Where? the railroad station ten miles away?"

"Yes," he said.

"You walked all that distance, then shoveled coal, and after that walked back? It is too much, and I am afraid you will get sick."

"I have danced all night many a time, and did n't get sick. I ought to be able to work as well as dance, eh? And here is a dollar to help pay for the new house," said he, proudly holding up the money.

"I remember the man at the station. He has a kind face," said I.

"But you should have seen him look at me when I went in last night and asked for work," said my father.

"What, you?" he said.

"Yes," I replied. "Can't you hire me to help shovel coal, like the man I see working out in the shed?"

"I thought you cared for nothing but dancing."

"I have given that up."

"What does all this mean?" he asked.

"My daughter has come home from Carlisle. I want to make money quick. I must have a better house for her to live in."

"You never shoveled coal, did you?"

"No," I replied, "but I believe I can."

"I need a man," he said. "I will pay you well if you work well."

"That was all I wanted," and he took a lantern,

and showed me what to do. Train after train came
in and took the coal from the bin, and it was my
work to fill up. Here is the dollar earned last
night. Put it in your trunk, and to-night I will
get another, maybe. We shall soon have our new
house, shan't we?" said he, looking as delighted
as any boy.

And to think that it was *my father* talking such
good common sense, — the man whom I did not
want to own as father when I first met him on my
return home, at that very station!

I did not see his Indian dress now. Not even
his coal-blacked face disturbed me.

My father had never been to school a day, yet behind his black eyes and down deep in his heart, I
saw in him the spirit which we at Carlisle had been
so earnestly advised to cultivate, — COURAGE.

CHAPTER XVI.

RESULTS.

We had many other seemingly unsurmountable difficulties to encounter in our progress up the hill of Right, but we soon found friends to help·us conquer some of our troubles.

My father continued to work and save his money until he had earned enough to build a comfortable adobe house with three rooms.

He adopted the civilized dress, with the exception of wearing short hair.

Although my mother never would change her Indian dress for one like mine, she was pleased to work as I did, and kept her house and the dishes nice and clean.

I worked with the trader's family until I had
enough money saved to buy necessary furnishings
for the house.

A few years after we were in the new home, two
of my Carlisle teachers came out to New Mexico
upon business for the school.

They stayed in our house, slept in my bed, now
an ash wood double-bed, and made up with as clean
white sheets as they had at Carlisle.

My teachers praised the Carlisle pictures and
others which adorned the wall, and spoke well of
the appearance of our best room, with its centre-
table and rocking-chair and other furniture.

When they saw my cousin's little girls wearing
nicely made dresses and aprons, and the little boys
in good fitting suits, all made by me on my new
sewing-machine; when they ate the bread and cake
and pie I baked, and the meat and eggs and potatoes

INDIAN SCHOOL, CARLISLE, PA

and cabbage and other good things I prepared and set before them on a table, spread with a clean table-cloth (a real one), and had napkins, too, they seemed so delighted that I felt more than repaid for the hard times I had passed through.

And, indeed, I have never regretted having braved the first hard steps that led me out of the accursed home slavery and made me a free woman.

If every returned girl could resist the first efforts of her home friends to drag her back into the old Indian ways, and make them feel in a kind but decided way that they were no longer right for her, she would eventually enjoy untold satisfaction and happiness.